THE PRINCE WON'T GO TO BED!

DAYLE ANN DODDS

Pictures by **KYRSTEN BROOKER**

Melanie Kroupa Books ✦ Farrar, Straus and Giroux ✦ New York

For Joey —D.D.

For my princes: John, Nicholas, and Kieran —K.B.

Text copyright © 2007 by Dayle Ann Dodds
Illustrations copyright © 2007 by Kyrsten Brooker
All rights reserved
Distributed in Canada by Douglas & McIntyre Ltd.
Color separations by Chroma Graphics PTE Ltd.
Printed and bound in China by South China Printing Co. Ltd.
Designed by Irene Metaxatos
First edition, 2007
1   3   5   7   9   10   8   6   4   2

www.fsgkidsbooks.com

Library of Congress Cataloging-in-Publication Data
Dodds, Dayle Ann.
   The prince won't go to bed / Dayle Ann Dodds ; pictures by Kyrsten Brooker.— 1st ed.
      p.   cm.
   Summary: When the young prince refuses to go to bed, assorted members of the
royal household offer their ideas on exactly what he needs, but it is his sister, Princess
Kate, who learns the truth.
   ISBN-13: 978-0-374-36108-2
   ISBN-10: 0-374-36108-8
   [1. Bedtime—Fiction. 2. Princes—Fiction. 3. Princesses—Fiction. 4. Stories in
rhyme.]   I. Brooker, Kyrsten, ill.   II. Title.

PZ8.3.D645 Pri 2007
[E]—dc22

2005051234

The castle was in trouble.
Nanny scratched her head.
"The King and Queen are at the ball,
and the Prince won't go to bed!"

She bounced the Prince upon her knee.
They played pat-patty-cake.

Then Nanny said, "Now go to sleep . . ."
That was her **BIG MISTAKE**.

For then . . .

"WAA! WAA! WAA!
I will not go to bed!"
the teeny-tiny, itty-bitty, little Prince said.

"He needs a nice warm **BATH**," suggested old Lord Gerty. "It's clear to me a prince can't sleep if he's soiled and dirty."

They RUB-DUBBED through the castle,
they RUB-DUBBED through the hall,
head to toe in bubbles,
Lord and Prince and all.

The happy Prince went back to bed.
No one heard a peep.
Nanny and Lord Gerty
tiptoed off to sleep.

But then . . .

"WAA! WAA! WAA! I will not go to bed!"

the teeny-tiny, itty-bitty, little Prince said.

"He needs a fluffy **PILLOW**," offered Squire Frat. "It's clear to me a prince can't sleep if his pillow's flat."

They FLEW around the castle,
they FLEW around the hall,
hanging on to pillows,
feathers, geese, and all.

The happy Prince went back to bed.
No one heard a peep.
Nanny, Lord, and Squire
tiptoed off to sleep.

But then . . .

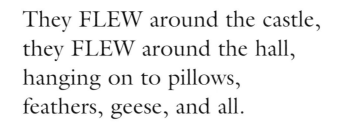

"WAA! WAA! WAA! I will not go to bed!"

the teeny-tiny, itty-bitty, little Prince said.

Said Cook, "He needs some **PUDDING**,
of peach and juicy plum.
It's clear to me the Prince can't sleep
until I make him some!"

They JIGGLED through the castle,
they JIGGLED through the hall,
carrying the pudding—
over three feet tall.

The happy Prince went back to bed.
No one heard a peep.
Nanny, Lord, Squire, and Cook
tiptoed off to sleep.

But then . . .

"WAA! WAA! WAA! I will not go to bed!"

the teeny-tiny, itty-bitty, little Prince said.

"Perhaps a softer **MATTRESS**?"
asked the Royal Guard.
"It's clear to me a prince can't sleep
when his bed's too hard."

They LEANED LEFT through the doorway,
they LEANED RIGHT through the hall,
balancing the mattresses,
twenty-two in all.

The happy Prince went back to bed.
No one heard a peep.
Nanny, Lord, Squire, Cook, and Guard
tiptoed off to sleep.

But then . . .

WAA! WAA! I will not go to bed!"

the teeny-tiny, itty-bitty, little Prince said.

"He needs some gentle **MUSIC**," sang Lady Lorali. "It's clear to me a prince can't sleep without a lullaby."

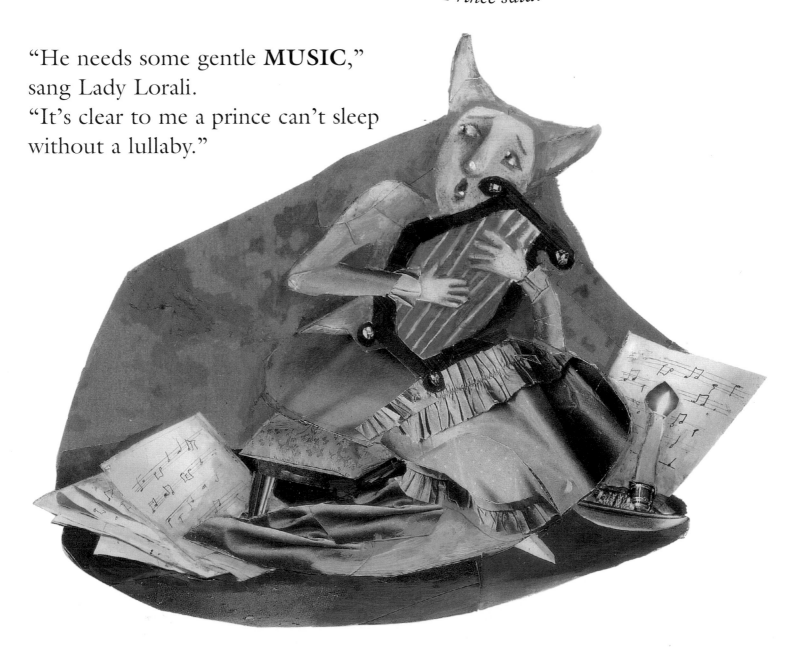

They STRUM-STRUMMED through the castle,
they PIPE-PIPED through the hall,
a band of court musicians,
bagpipes, lute, and all.

The happy Prince went back to bed.
No one heard a peep.
Nanny, Cook, and all the rest
tiptoed off to sleep.

But then . . .

"WAA! WAA! WAA!

I will not go to bed!"

the teeny-tiny, itty-bitty, little Prince said.

"There must be *something* we forgot."
Nanny scratched her head.
"For it's clear, the little Prince just

WILL NOT GO TO BED!"

Down the hall, Princess Kate
awoke from all the clatter,
and hurried to her brother's room
in slippers, *pitter-patter*.

She put her brother on her knee
and said, "What's wrong, my dear?"
The teeny-tiny little Prince
whispered in her ear.

Kate smiled and faced the Royal Court.
"You see, the truth is this.
You have thought of *everything*,
except . . . a **GOOD-NIGHT KISS**."

She tucked the Prince back into bed.
No one heard a peep.

For the teeny-tiny little Prince

had fallen

fast asleep.